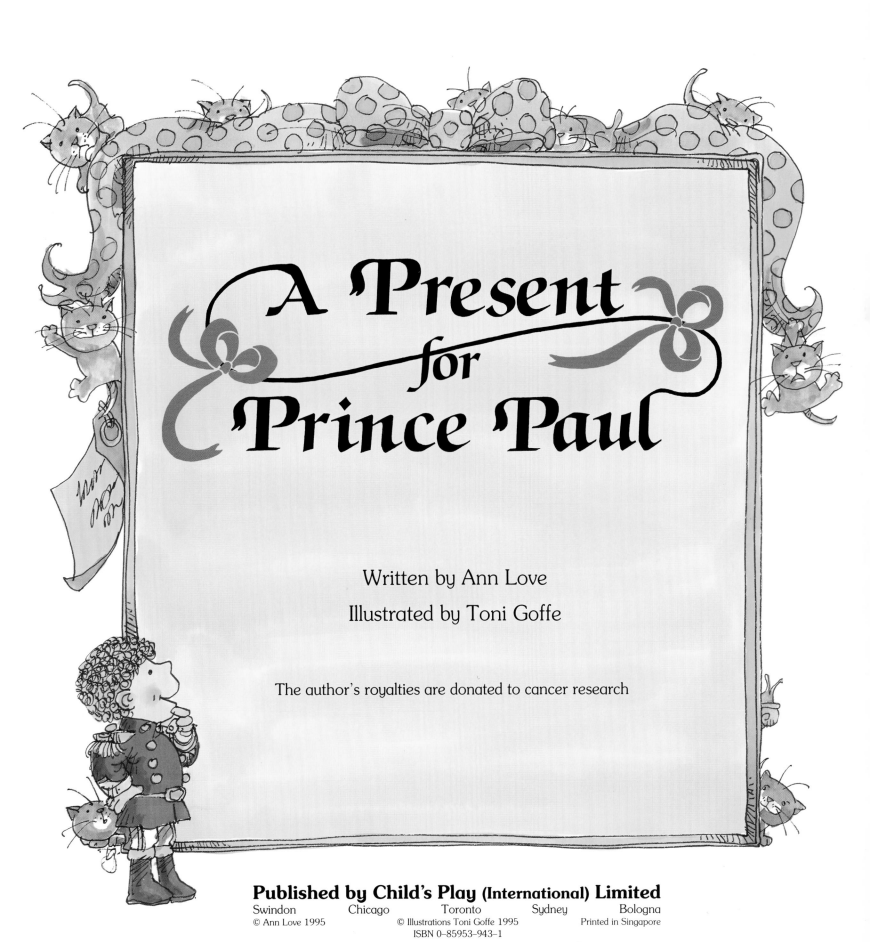

A Present for Prince Paul

Written by Ann Love

Illustrated by Toni Goffe

The author's royalties are donated to cancer research

Published by Child's Play (International) Limited

Swindon   Chicago   Toronto   Sydney   Bologna

© Ann Love 1995   © Illustrations Toni Goffe 1995   Printed in Singapore

ISBN 0–85953–943–1

A catalogue reference for this book is available from the British Library

"What ever is the matter?" screamed the queen one morning, as her husband, kind, normally calm, King Clifford, dropped the breakfast tray.

"It's the Court Journal, my Love. It seems there are only three days to Prince Paul's sixth birthday. What are we going to do? Shall we hold a grand parade? I could review the troops."

"Certainly not!" replied the queen. "A garden party is what is required. I will invite all the nobility and wear my best party gown."

"I don't think the Prince will like that," muttered the king.

"In that case," retorted the queen sharply. "Why don't you ask him what he would like?"

"My Dove!" exclaimed the king. "That is a really good idea!"

"For once," he added under his breath.

He found the prince in the castle kitchen,
talking to his friend Jim,
the son of the castle cook.

"Prince Paul," said the king. "The Queen and I
have been discussing your birthday celebrations.
Is there anything special you would like?"

The prince looked pleased.
"Thank you, Father," he said.
"Please, may I talk it over with Jim
and let you know?"

"Of course," replied the king.
"But don't take too long.
There are a lot of arrangements
to make."

All that day, Prince Paul and Jim thought about the matter. In the afternoon, they crossed the valley to the next kingdom to ask Prince Peter what he thought.

Prince Peter is Prince Paul's very best friend.

They ate supper with Peter's wise, old grandmother, and, while they were there, they reached a decision.

On his return, Prince Paul
went straight to tell King Clifford.

"Father," he said. "I know what I want for my birthday.
Please, may I have a ball?"

"Splendid idea!" exclaimed the king.
"Why didn't the Queen and I think of that?
It will suit us both just fine!
Now, what sort of ball would you like?
A small one, I suppose, for you and your friends?"

"No, Father. Actually, I would like it
to be quite large."

"Whatever you wish," said the king.
"Of course, the court musicians will play."

The prince frowned. "Really, Father?
I don't think they will be much good."

"Don't be unkind, my boy.
I know what you mean,
but they will have plenty of time to practise."

"You and your friends will need a coach, too,"
the king added.

"Don't worry about that, Father," said the prince.
"Jim will look after all that."

The king looked surprised.
Everyone said that Jim was lazy.

"One job less for me," said the king.
"I must remember to compliment cook
on the helpfulness of her son.
Well, I had better get started.
We have only forty-eight hours to prepare.

"But first I must tell your Mother the good news."

The queen was delighted.

"Our little boy is growing up.
We must invite Princess Eleanor and her friends
for him to dance with."

"Mother and I will look after the really difficult jobs,
like trying on dresses and planning the guest list.
It is so important deciding who to leave out."

She sent the king to take care of everything else.

First, he searched for the court musicians.

They hadn't been seen since the feast
to celebrate the birth of Prince Paul.

He found them in a turret high in the castle.

They and their instruments
were in a dreadful state of neglect.
The king ordered them to prepare for the ball.

Next, he hurried to see the castle cook.

Hot and tired after a busy day,
the cook was not at all pleased
to be handed the long list of food
which would be needed for the ball.

"How am I to do this in forty-eight hours?"
she grumbled.

"I am sure Jim will help you," said the king.
"He is such a capable lad."

The cook thought the king was making fun
of her son. Jim was certainly capable,
but helping in the kitchen was not his strong point.

"How could you?" she cried, bursting into tears.
"I can feel one of my migraines coming on."

The king knew what that meant
and hurried back to report to the queen.

The queen and queen mother were busy trying on dresses.
As they did so, they discussed the guest list.

"We shall have to invite Prince Peter and his parents,"
said the queen. "And his grandmother."

"Oh, we can't invite her!" the queen mother exclaimed.
"Just sits around knitting all day, poor old thing.
No wonder, she is so woolly-minded.
I have never knitted a stitch in my entire life."

"Excuse me, my Dear," said the king,
when he managed to get a word in.
"I seem to have upset cook
and she has taken to her bed.
Do you think you and Queen Mother
can look after the food?"

"Can't you see how busy we are?" snorted the queen.
"Go and get on with it! … Men!"

There was nothing left for it.
The king summoned the general.

For the next two days,
the soldiers worked with military precision
to prepare food for the ball.

At last, the big day arrived.

As soon as he awoke, Prince Paul ran to find his parents.
His eye roved over a pile of cards on the breakfast table.

"Happy birthday!" cried the king and queen,
as they embraced their son.

"Happy birthday!" echoed the queen mother.
"Come and see what your Granny has brought you."

She gave him a sloppy wet kiss, which he wiped off
when she wasn't looking.

Then she handed the prince a square-shaped parcel.

Inside was a dictionary with a label which read:
   "*A prince who can read needs lots of proper nouns.*"

"Thank you, Granny. I'll start reading tomorrow."

Then, with a puzzled look, Prince Paul asked,
"When may I have my ball?"

"In the hall at five o'clock," beamed the queen proudly.

"Oh, great!" exclaimed Prince Paul, looking relieved.
He ran off to spend the rest of the day with his friends.

At five o'clock, all the guests
were gathered in the great hall.
The court musicians began to play
'Happy Birthday, Prince Paul'.

The sound of music faded and a gasp went up,
as the great doors opened and in trotted
Prince Paul and Prince Peter and their friends,
dressed in shorts and striped jerseys.

The queen mother turned pale
and grasped her smelling salts.

"Whatever have you got on?" she asked.

"Our soccer strip," replied Prince Paul.
"Prince Peter's granny invented
this new football game called soccer
and knitted the jerseys for us.
Isn't she great?"

Princess Eleanor began to giggle.

"What is she doing here?"
asked Prince Paul, his face turning red.

"Princess Eleanor,"
said the king sternly,
"is your dancing partner
at your BIRTHDAY BALL."

Prince Paul's little face
was beginning to pucker.

"BIRTHDAY BALL …?" he quivered.
"That's not the sort of ball I wanted.

"Now, we'll never get to play soccer."

"Oh, yes, you will!" said Peter's granny,
holding up a huge ball made of wool.

"I knitted this specially.
It is ideal for playing indoors.
Happy Birthday!

"You and your friends will play ball, after all!"

"Oh, NO, you won't,"
said the queen mother.
"Princess Eleanor and her friends
want to dance!"

"Oh, YES, you will!"
said Princess Eleanor.
"WE want to play soccer, too!
Don't we?"

"YES!" chorused all the girls.

"And we can dance afterwards,"
said Prince Paul.

Everybody had fun.

The court ladies forgot
about their fine dresses.

Even the queen mother
stopped remembering
how important she was.

They played soccer
until the ball unravelled.

Then they danced, young and old.
The court musicians were in top form.

When they were tired,
they went down into the cellar
and tucked into the feast
prepared by the troops.

Nobody thought about bedtime.

At last, the cook,
who had recovered her good humour,
brought in a very unusual birthday cake
which Jim had helped her bake.

"How will we avoid making
such a silly mistake next year?"
asked the king.

"I know," said Prince Paul.
We'll play soccer every year
on my birthday!"